JAMES STEVENSON

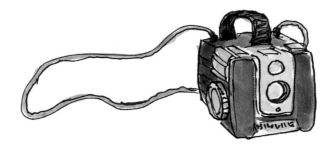

GREENWILLOW BOOKS
An Imprint of HarperCollins*Publishers*

For Susan Hirschman,
with love

The Castaway
Copyright © 2002 by James Stevenson
All rights reserved. Printed in Hong Kong by South China Printing Co. (1988) Ltd.
www.harperchildrens.com

Watercolor paints and a black pen were used to prepare the full-color art.

Library of Congress Cataloging-in-Publication Data

Stevenson, James, (date)
The castaway / by James Stevenson.
p.   cm.
"Greenwillow Books."
Summary: During a family vacation, Hubie the mouse falls out of a
dirigible and is stranded on a tropical island, where a very inventive
fellow castaway, Leo, helps him overcome his fears.
ISBN 0-688-16965-1 (trade). ISBN 0-688-16966-X (lib. bdg.)
[1. Castaways—Fiction. 2. Islands—Fiction. 3. Vacations—Fiction.
4. Mice—Fiction. 5. Porcupines—Fiction. 6. Cartoons and comics.]
I. Title.   PZ7.S84748 Cas 2002   [E]—dc21   2001033826

First Edition 10 9 8 7 6 5 4 3 2 1